ONE-MINUTE
BIRTHDAY
STORIES

ONE-MINUTE BIRTHDAY STORIES

Shari Lewis
and
Lan O'Kun

ILLUSTRATED BY
RICHARD REHBEIN

A DOUBLEDAY BOOK FOR YOUNG READERS

To my friend and editor Wendy Barish,
who has helped conceive and give birth
to so many of these One-Minute storybooks.

A Doubleday Book For Young Readers

PUBLISHED BY DELACORTE PRESS
Bantam Doubleday Dell Publishing Group, Inc.
666 Fifth Avenue, New York, New York 10103

DOUBLEDAY
and the portrayal of an anchor with a dolphin
are trademarks of Bantam Doubleday Dell Publishing Group, Inc.

Research assistant, Stephanie Carbone

Library of Congress Cataloging-in-Publication Data
Lewis, Shari.
One-minute birthday stories / written and adapted by
Shari Lewis and Lan O'Kun; illustrated by
Richard Rehbein. — 1st ed.
p.   cm.
Summary: A collection of twenty stories about
birthdays, designed to be read or told in a minute or less.
1. Birthdays — Juvenile fiction.   2. Children's stories,
American.   [1. Birthdays — Fiction.   2. Short stories.]
I. O'Kun, Lan.   II. Rehbein, Richard, ill.   III. Title.
PZ5.L6Onb   1991
[E] — dc20   90-3641   CIP   AC

ISBN 0-385-41325-4
RL: 3.1
Printed in the United States of America
March 1992

10 9 8 7 6 5 4 3 2 1
WOR

Contents

Introduction

Everyone yearns to be special. From the moment you celebrate your first birthday, you recognize that on this day, at the very least, you are *it!*

Birthdays are also important to kids because they recognize that each birthday is a clear marker on the path to adulthood.

Most often, the birthdays we celebrate (and those we see celebrated by the people around us) are very much the same, made up of parties and cakes and (if we're lucky) gifts.

This book is full of stories to provide your youngsters with other perspectives on birthdays: how they are experienced by people with other points of view—a homeless child, a lonely one, a small boy in ancient Egypt and a youth who, having reached a long-awaited birthday, sets off on an adventure.

Your birthday child will hear what happened to The Little Lame Prince, and to a lucky kid who gets to spend his birthday with a friendly giant.

Here you will find one birthday viewed from great age, and another experienced by one of great fame (all about the time Shirley Temple turned nine).

Of course, there *was* a time when only rulers could celebrate their birthdays. In temples, people would light candles for their kings and pharaohs, offer them fruit and cakes, and commend them happily to the gods. Through the years, these religious rituals have become part of our personal yearly rite of passage: the cakes, candles, the gifts and the good wishes.

And here, you have *our* best wishes and stories. Happy Birthday, everybody!

Love,
Shari Lewis and
Lan O'Kun

How Bugaboo Got His Cake Made

Bugaboo sat stirring his pan near a fire. "What are you making, Bugaboo?" asked Mr. Bearly.

"My birthday cake," Bugaboo replied.

Mr. Bearly peered into the pan and laughed. "You've only got nuts in that pan."

Bugaboo smiled a secret smile and said, "It's going to be a nutty cake."

"It's not going to be a cake at all," Mr. Bearly insisted. "You don't have any flour in there."

"Or milk," said Don Swan, who just happened to waddle by.

Now Bugaboo *knew* that he needed flour and milk, but he didn't have money for flour or milk or anything else!

"You need butter, too," suggested Grizzly.

"And sugar," added ToothPig.

"And chocolate icing," said Tilly Goat. "I'd love to taste your birthday cake, if it had chocolate icing."

"Oh no!" declared Bugaboo. "If I make this nutty cake all by myself, I'll *eat* it all by myself. No one can share my cake who doesn't chip in!"

Bugaboo giggled to himself and stirred his pot of nuts as his friends ran out the door. In a few minutes, Mr. Bearly returned with flour. Don Swan swam over with milk. Grizzly brought butter. ToothPig added sugar, and Tilly Goat gave Bugaboo a bowl full of chocolate icing.

Bugaboo mixed together all the goodies his friends had brought and baked his cake. As he spread the icing, he said, "Welcome to my party —enjoy my delicious home-baked cake."

"Isn't that Bugaboo silly?" remarked Tilly Goat as they left Bugaboo's birthday party. "If it weren't for us, Bugaboo wouldn't have had a cake at all!"

But Bugaboo just laughed. "You are all invited over for lemonade next week," he called. "I already have the water!"

The Agreement

"**W**hat shall I give you for your birthday?" asked Grandpa as they waited for the party guests to arrive.

"I hate my birthday," Charley Bonny said unhappily. "February twenty-ninth is an awful day to be born on. I'm eight years old and I've only had two actual birthdays. I'm really only *two*." (Just in case

you didn't know it, February is the only month in the year that usually has twenty-eight days, instead of thirty or thirty-one. Every four years, though, February has a twenty-ninth day . . . and that is the day Charley Bonny was born. You can see Charley's problem.)

"You're a big boy for two," Grandpa Bonny said, trying to get a smile out of Charley. "That bike Daddy got you is too big for a two-year-old." Charley didn't smile. "Listen, I envy you," Grandpa said. "I turned seventy on August thirteenth. I certainly wish I could stay seventy for another four years."

Suddenly Grandpa knew what he was going to give Charley as a birthday present. "Tell you what. I'm going to give you my birthday."

"You can't do that," Charley said.

"It's my birthday. I can do what I want with it," Grandpa replied.

"But what'll we do with *mine?*"

"*I'll* take yours. We'll swap. That way I'll get old *slower*—only one birthday every four years, which will suit me—and you'll get older *faster*, with a birthday every year, which will suit *you.*" Luckily Grandpa was a lawyer, and he knew how to make these things official. He wrote out the agreement and they both signed it.

Charley became nine the very next year, on August thirteenth. And Grandpa? Why, he turned seventy-one—on February twenty-ninth, four years later.

Swallow

Some insects have six legs. Some insects have eight legs. Clara, the centipede, had so many legs that she never learned to count how many she had. In fact, when somebody would ask her she'd say, "Oh, I have a hundred legs," because a hundred is certainly a great many legs.

What was awful was that Clara had sore feet. How many? "Oh, I have fifty-eight sore feet," she'd say—though she never really counted —"and with my birthday coming up, the best present I could ask for is that my fifty-eight feet wouldn't hurt anymore."

"You ought to see a doctor," Amy Ant said to her. "I recommend Barney Bee." It took four hours for Dr. Bee to examine all fifty-eight legs. But at last he said, "Clara my dear, you ought to get off your feet."

"My birthday is coming," she said. "That would be the day to do it."

Well, if you've got two legs, getting off your feet is easy. But if you're an insect with a *hundred*—why, you've got legs *everywhere.*

"I'll get you off your feet," said Sidney Swallow, a bird who happened to be flying by. "On the morning of your birthday, as a present, I will pick you up and carry you around in my beak."

True to his word, the Swallow came to the centipede's nest, wished Clara a happy birthday, picked her up in his beak and flew away with her. Unfortunately, the bird ate her for breakfast.

"In one gulp?" Amy Ant asked.

"No," replied Dr. Bee. "In one *swallow.*"

Willy Will

On the day that Willy Will was born, a bird was born, too, on the windowsill outside Willy's nursery. The North Wind said to itself, "I do not know what this means, but I feel it is a good sign."

The next year, on the same day on which it was born, something made the bird return to Willy Will's windowsill, after a long journey from the South. The child was delighted, and his mother declared that nothing they had bought Willy for his first birthday was as good a present as the little bird.

And for five years, the bird returned on the day of its birth to that windowsill. Each year Willy looked forward to its coming, and each year the North Wind stayed long enough to see the child's happiness.

Two weeks before his sixth birthday, Willy Will became very sick. Through the window, the North Wind saw the pale child grow weaker each day. So the North Wind blew south, found the little bird and told him the sad news.

"I'm too old to fly north this year," moaned the bird. The North Wind urged, "Take to the sky and I will carry you along. Try!" The bird did, and the Wind stayed under its wings for the entire journey. It arrived at the windowsill five days early. When Willy Will saw the bird, he began to feel better, and by his birthday he was well enough to go out and play. But the bird was exhausted from the trip.

"I cannot fly anymore," he told the North Wind. "And if I cannot fly, I will die."

"Spread your wings and I will take you higher than any bird has ever flown."

The little bird did as he was told, and the North Wind blew him up, up, up among the stars, where he lived happily—and forever— after.

The Little Lame Prince

Long ago a great stone tower was built in a spot that was absolutely nowhere. At the top of the tower lived a crippled little boy and an old woman who took care of him. The boy could not walk, but even if he could, there were no steps leading down from the top of the tower to the ground, so there was no escape for them. Once a week, a knight on a black horse would ride to the base of the tower. The old woman would lower a basket on a rope, and the knight would fill it with food and ride away.

The boy, who was really a prince, had secretly been tucked

away in this tower when he was a baby by his wicked uncle, who had ruled over the prince's lands for all the years since. This uncle was very cruel and the people in the kingdom hated him, but he had lied to them and said that the little prince had *died* just after he was born, so no one knew about the awful tower.

The queen of the fairies took pity on the suffering people of the kingdom. On the morning of the prince's tenth birthday, he awoke to find the tiny woman sitting on his bed. "Little prince, your people need you," she said, spreading a magic cloak on the floor. The minute the bewildered boy crawled onto it, the cloak rose, flew out of the tower and through the air to what was rightfully the little prince's castle. It swished through a window of the throne room with the boy and settled right upon the throne itself. When the mean uncle saw his nephew on the throne, he was terrified. He told the prince he was sorry, begged his forgiveness, and gave him back the kingdom, which the little lame prince ruled wonderfully and wisely for the rest of his life.

How is *that* for a tenth birthday present?

Happy Birthday, Darling

Martha opened her eyes and looked into her mother's face. "Happy Birthday, darling," Mother whispered.

"I'm five," Martha said, and sat up. She'd never been able to say that before. Now she saw that there were gifts piled at the foot of her bed.

"How's my five-year-old?" asked Daddy with a big grin.

"Fine," she said, feeling *really* fine. What a day it was! She opened eight presents, squealing happily with each one, and especially loudly for the last—a doll carriage that she had been wanting for months.

At her birthday party that afternoon, Snooksey the clown tickled her. Her thirteen best friends were there, and they had ice-cream cake and made lots of noise, and played games and ran around. . . . And then it was over.

That night, when the lights were out, Martha thought about her wonderful fifth birthday. "Darn," she said to herself. "It's over." She shut her eyes and tried to sleep. But she kept thinking about her special day, and repeating to herself, "Darn. Why does my birthday have to be over? Why can you get to be five on only *one day?*"

"Happy Birthday, darling." Mother said. Martha opened her eyes.

"I'm five," Martha said—and this time she *was*. She had dreamed her entire birthday, and now here it was again, for her to enjoy a second time!

Manhood

In Egypt five thousand years ago, children's birthdays were not celebrated. But Put was about to be twelve years old, and twelve was the beginning of manhood. "I am a lucky fellow," Put said to himself, "because my birthday is on the fifth day of the month, the same as the birthday of the god Ptolemy."

Put's father bought a cow at the market to be killed and eaten for Put's birthday supper. When Put saw the cow his heart went out to it.

"Father, I do not want to eat this cow. I want her as a pet."

"You are obviously still a child," his father said. "Cows are not pets." Put ran to the temple and prayed to Ptolemy.

"It is our birthday today," he said tearfully. "Please make a miracle and spare my cow."

When Put got back to the farm something was wrong with the cow. Put shouted for his father to come, but although he was working in a field nearby, he didn't seem to hear Put's frantic calls. Then the cow began to give birth. It was having a lot of trouble, and without Put's help both the calf and the mother cow would surely have died.

Later, when his father came to kill the cow and cook it, he saw Put holding the new calf.

"A child could not have done what I have done," Put said.

"Agreed," replied his father with pride. "This is a man's work."

"Then, if I am a man, I will decide what shall become of my cow." And he whispered, "Thank you, Ptolemy."

And that was how a birthday meal became two birthday presents.

Banbury Cross

There was an old lady, as everyone knows,
Who had rings on her fingers and bells on her toes.
She lived in a town known as Banbury Cross—
Don't ask me where that was, for I'm at a loss.
But people there knew the old lady of course
For the music her bells made, and for her white horse,
Who had bells on his nose and three bells on each ear
That would jingle as well, when she would appear.
The grandchild she loved was a fine little boy,
And when he was five Grandma sent him a toy,
A cock-horse—a pole with a horse's head.
"Happy Birthday, my darling!" the card inside read.
"Quick, gallop to see me," his grandmother wrote,
"I've got a surprise for you," ended the note.
He left after breakfast, rode all afternoon,
And arrived at the rise of a bright yellow moon.

There he saw Grandma, who blew him a kiss,
And said from her saddle, "Just listen to this!
My horse and I practiced as never before
To give you this gift." And without saying more
The horse began dancing; the bells on his nose
Blended with those on the tips of her toes,
And the bells on his tail all ring-rang as they swayed,
And what a surprise! Not just *jingling* they made
But a song that the little boy instantly knew,
"Happy Birthday, my darling, Happy Birthday to you!"

The Unhappiest Birthday

When Charles Dickens was very young his father pointed out a wealthy man's house and said to his son, "If you learn a lot, and work very hard, someday you could own a home like that one."

Charles, remembering his father's words, worked very hard indeed, just as he saw his father do. Yet his Dad, for all of his hard work, lost his job, and—as happened in England in those days to people who could not pay their bills—he went to jail.

Since the family no longer had any money, Charles was taken out of school, and on his twelfth birthday he was sent to work in a dark factory where they made ink. There he toiled twelve hours every day of the week, and he was beaten if he fell asleep while working. He was filthy and afraid all the time. But the worst thing was that he could no longer go to school—and he knew that if he could not learn anything, he would never be able to get a better job.

One day his father was released from jail. He took his son out of the factory and somehow managed to send the boy back to school. But Charles Dickens never forgot what had happened to him on his twelfth birthday. He worked hard for the rest of his life: in fact, he became one of the greatest writers of all time, and is remembered especially for his books about poor boys whose families had fallen on hard times, like David Copperfield, Oliver Twist, and Tiny Tim.

Oh, yes . . . one day when Charles Dickens was a father himself, he was able to buy the very house his father had pointed out to him!

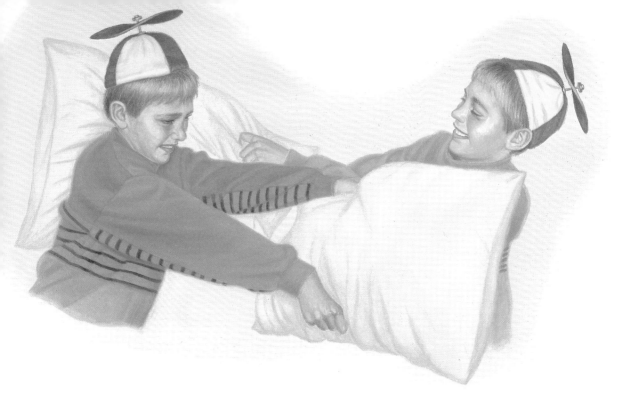

"I Was Born First"

Tweedledum and Tweedledee were twin brothers who were—as twins always are—born one right after the other.

"I was born first," said Tweedledum.

"Maybe before somebody else. But not before me," said Tweedledee.

"My birthday is September fourth," said Tweedledum.

"*My* birthday is September fourth," said Tweedledee, and he picked up Tweedledum's rattle and broke it.

"Let's fight about it," said Tweedledum, looking at his broken rattle.

"All right," said Tweedledee, and he picked up a pillow.

"Since I was born first I get to hit you first," said Tweedledum. "Give me the pillow." Tweedledee was about to give Tweedledum the pillow right in the nose when the biggest crow you ever saw flew past their window. It was so big that Tweedledum and Tweedledee ran under their beds and hid.

"Did you see that big crow?" asked Tweedledum. "It scared me."

"Scared me first," said Tweedledee.

"It scared me before it scared you," said Tweedledum. "Now what were we going to fight about?"

"I forgot," said Tweedledum.

"I forgot first," said Tweedledee.

"Does it matter?" said Tweedledum.

"No," said Tweedledee. "Let's fight tomorrow, when we remember."

But they never did remember so they never did fight, and that is the end of the story. All that's left is the poem from Mother Goose:

> Tweedledum and Tweedledee
> Resolved to have a battle
> For Twecdledum said Tweedledee
> Had spoiled his nice new rattle.
> Just then flew by a monstrous crow,
> As big as a tar barrel
> Which frightened both the heroes so,
> They quite forgot their quarrel.

Nobody's Birthday

The only thing they were sure of was that he was a puppy. He certainly wasn't a collie. He wasn't a poodle, either. He was neither a fox terrier nor a cocker spaniel, but he might have had any of those breeds in him. Then again, he might have had none of *them*, but bits and pieces of *other* breeds instead.

The pup had followed Teddy home one day. He looked so bedraggled and sad, the family decided to keep him. They didn't know anything about him, and didn't know who to ask. Teddy called his new dog "Nobody."

They figured that Nobody was about a year old. He was a good sweet doggy. He didn't bark a lot, and he minded his own business.

Teddy decided to welcome Nobody to the house by giving him a birthday party, so the boy called a bunch of his friends and invited them to celebrate his new dog's first birthday.

They all asked the same question. "Who's coming?"

"The only thing I'm sure of," said Teddy, "is that Nobody'll be there."

Well, that didn't sound like much fun to Teddy's friends, so on the day of the party, nobody came!

There were party hats and favors and a cake, but no guests.

Teddy knew just what to do. Right then and there, he changed his dog's name. "Everybody," that's what he named him.

Then Teddy raced to the phone. "You're missing the dog's birthday party. Why don't you come, quick!"

Teddy's pals asked, "Who's there?"

"Everybody!" shouted Teddy, "just Everybody."

All of Teddy's friends hurried to the house—and they could see that Teddy was right. Everybody *was* there.

And guess who had the best time at the party?

Everybody!

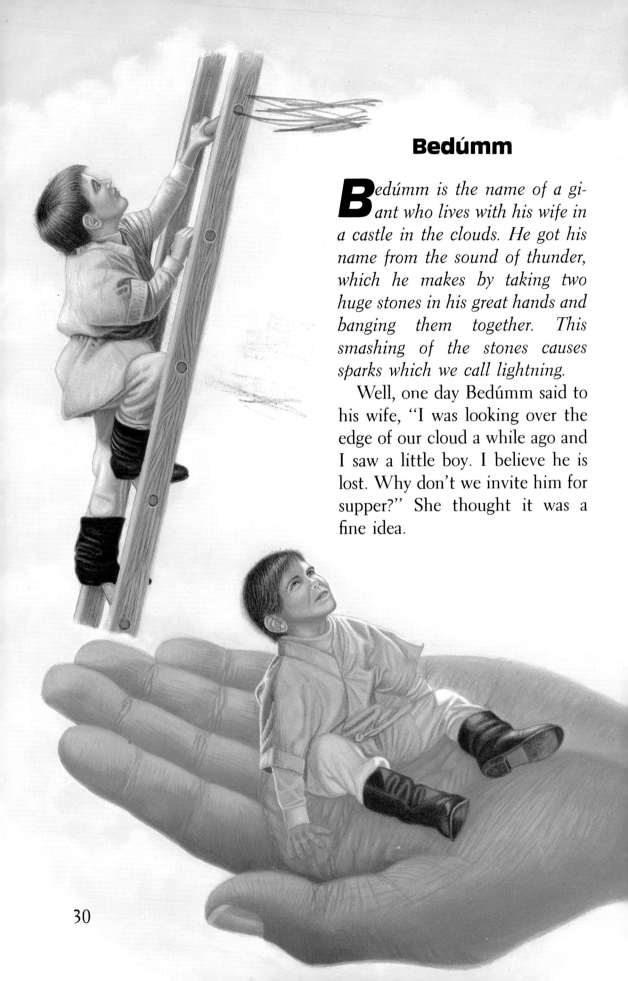

Bedúmm

Bedúmm is the name of a gi-ant who lives with his wife in a castle in the clouds. He got his name from the sound of thunder, which he makes by taking two huge stones in his great hands and banging them together. This smashing of the stones causes sparks which we call lightning.

Well, one day Bedúmm said to his wife, "I was looking over the edge of our cloud a while ago and I saw a little boy. I believe he is lost. Why don't we invite him for supper?" She thought it was a fine idea.

The little boy, David, was indeed lost. His mother had taken him to their village to buy a present for his birthday, and while she was shopping, she'd left David waiting outside the store.

"Don't move," she had said, but David hadn't listened. Now, wandering on a country road, he was surprised to see a ladder hanging from a great cloud above him. Full of wonder, David began to climb the ladder. Up and up and up he went and right on through the cloud, where Bedúmm stood waiting for him. The giant smiled, and, putting David in the palm of his hand, carried him carefully to his castle. There the giant's wife had prepared a wonderful soup of raindrops, which she served the boy from her thimble. When he discovered that it was David's birthday, Bedúmm made the loudest thunder and the brightest lightning anyone had ever seen, especially in David's honor. David was so delighted that the giant vowed that ever after, whenever he made thunder and lightning, he would invite a birthday child to come and see.

So, the next time you see lightning flash, followed by a huge *BEDÚMM* . . . you'll know that some child is having a birthday party in the sky.

Anything You Set Your Mind To

Terry Brink could not learn to swim. He had been trying since he was very little, but the water didn't seem to hold him up. Everybody else floated. Terry sank. It made no sense. He went to the big pool. There, everybody swam except him—or so it seemed.

"What is wrong with me?" he muttered.

"There's nothing wrong with you," the lifeguard replied. "Keep trying." Terry Brink kept trying—and he kept sinking. When his

father asked him what he wanted for his seventh birthday, Terry said, "I want to be able to swim."

Terry's dad assured him, "You can do anything you set your mind to."

"I can do anything I set my mind to," Terry Brink repeated to himself.

Early on the morning of Terry's seventh birthday, Terry's mom and dad got the best swimming teacher they could find, and took their birthday boy to the pool. Terry worked and played with the teacher almost all day. Terry blew bubbles. He kicked his feet. He used his arms. First he found that he could stay afloat in one place by using his arms and legs to tread water, and then—suddenly—he was swimming. What had seemed impossible until this particular day suddenly happened! Terry Brink swam across the pool.

"You see," his dad said. "You can do anything you set your mind to."

Terry Brink grinned. "Dad," he said, "for my *eighth* birthday, I want to fly!"

Humpty Dumpty Through the Looking Glass

The mirror over the fireplace had somehow gotten soft, so Alice had walked through it. And that afternoon she met an egg named Humpty Dumpty, sitting on a wall, wearing a green belt.

"What a beautiful belt," said Alice.

"It was an un-birthday present from the King and Queen," Humpty Dumpty replied.

"What is an un-birthday present?" Alice asked.

"A present given when it isn't your birthday, of course," Humpty Dumpty said. Alice considered that. "I like birthdays best," she replied at last.

"How many days are there in a year?" Humpty asked.

"Three hundred and sixty-five," Alice responded.

"And how many birthdays have you?" Humpty inquired.

"One."

"Well," Humpty Dumpty snickered, "there are three hundred and sixty-*four* days when you might expect un-birthday presents and only *one* day for birthday presents. Give me an *un*-birthday any time!"

Alice didn't know what to say. Humpty Dumpty grinned. "Do you realize you've lost an argument with an egg?" he asked, and he laughed so hard he fell off the wall and broke into thirty-two pieces. And all the King's horses and all the King's men arrived, but they couldn't put him back together again.

Oh, but you know that part.

Teddy and Teddy

Once upon a time there was a President of the United States whose nickname was Teddy. His real name was Theodore, but Teddy was what everyone called him. Just like Teddy bear. Of course, this President's last name wasn't Bear. It was Roosevelt, but he had once saved the life of a little bear, and when a toy company made a fuzzy, stuffed toy bear, they called it Teddy, after President Teddy Roosevelt.

Lots of boys are named Teddy, too, and when one of them, Teddy Tillson, was two years old, he had a birthday party. His cousin Barbara gave him one of those stuffed Teddy bears and said, "Teddy is a very important name. There are two famous Teddys that *I* know of. One is Teddy Roosevelt and the other is Teddy bear. I couldn't get Teddy Roosevelt to come and see you, but I've brought you Teddy bear."

Soon afterward, cousin Barbara moved far away. She didn't see Teddy Tillson for a few years. When she met him next, it was at the boy's fifth birthday party.

"What do you want to be when you grow up?" asked cousin Barbara.

Teddy Tillson replied, "I want to be another famous Teddy."

Barbara was impressed. "So," she said, "you want to be President of the United States?"

"No." The boy smiled. "I want to be a bear!"

When She Was Nine

Most children dream of what they want to become when they grow up. Shirley Temple didn't wait until she was grown up—she began to sing and dance in the movies when she was three years old.

In 1933, Shirley Temple, who was then five, was making one hundred and fifty dollars a week.

When Shirley Temple was six, she made *seven* motion pictures in one year, many more than any star makes today.

By 1935, seven-year-old Shirley was *the* most popular movie star in the world. That year she received the first Academy Award ever won by a child. The award—

Y W O O D

a golden statue called an OSCAR —came with a card that read: "Shirley Temple has brought more happiness to millions of children and grown-ups than any other child in the history of the world."

At eight, Shirley Temple was the seventh-highest-paid person in the United States.

And, for Shirley Temple's ninth birthday party, her loving fans sent more than one hundred and thirty *thousand* presents, including hundreds of dolls and a live baby kangaroo.

For *my* birthday that year, I got *one* doll, and my parents took me to see a Shirley Temple movie.

Twenty-one

There was once a poor farmer who had three sons. But only the youngest did any work. The oldest two, who were twins, sat around making fun of their little brother. They spoke of nothing but the gold they would find out in the world when they became "men" of twenty-one.

At last their twenty-first birthday arrived. Before their father or brother had arisen, the two worthless fellows packed some bread in a knapsack—for that's all the food there was in the house—and, carry-

ing two flasks of water, sneaked away. When their father awoke and found them gone, he wept. A year passed and the brothers did not return. Their father's hair went white with worry.

When the youngest boy turned twenty-one he hugged his father. "I cannot bear to see your unhappiness," he sighed. "I will find my brothers." Carrying only bread and water (as his brothers had), he set out. He had not gone far when he met a tiny man with a long white beard. "I am hungry and thirsty," the old man said. "Have you anything for me?" The young man immediately gave his bread and his flask of water to the bearded one. "Take it all," he said. The old man smiled, ate and drank, and then pulled two toads from his pocket. "These are your brothers," he said. "They have become what they actually always were. They shared nothing they had, but tried to steal my gold. Take them back to your poor father. And here, take this." He produced a sack of gold from under his coat and gave it to the young man. "It's yours to do with as you see fit."

As the youngest brother passed through the door at home, the enchantment was broken and his two brothers stood beside him. They hung their heads, but he happily embraced them, and since the older boys had learned their lesson, the family lived together in peace and kindness forevermore.

The Woman Who Never Moved

Charley Jarrow, who was eight, read about the old woman in the newspaper. The article said that Mrs. May Cuddles had turned one hundred years old that day, and now she sat on her porch and never said a word to anybody—nor did she ever move.

"Why, that lady lives just down by Four Corners," Charley Jarrow said to his dad. "I'm going to visit her. I never saw anybody that *never moves.*"

His dad smiled. "She's a hundred. That's why she never moves. She's *done* all her moving, I expect." But Charley Jarrow got it into his mind that everybody should move, a hundred or not. "She never says anything to anybody," he thought to himself. "Maybe it's because she doesn't have anybody to say anything *to.* I'll just go look her up. Heck, I'll bet I can get her moving." And so Charley hiked three miles to her house. Sure enough, there was the woman on the porch, just as the article had said. He climbed the steps, but she paid no attention to him.

"I understand you are ninety-six years old," Charley said. The old lady's eyes popped open.

"One hundred. Ask anybody."

"Nobody knows for sure," the boy commented.

"Ovie Wumpum knows."

Charley shrugged. "I don't know Ovie Wumpum."

"He lives down the road. About a mile," insisted Mrs. Cuddles.

"Well, I don't know . . ." Charley began. But Mrs. Cuddles got up creakily out of her chair, threw off the blankets, took his hand, and they began walking. It took a long time for May Cuddles and Charley Jarrow to walk the mile to Ovie Wumpum's place and back, but she made it.

"Best birthday I've had in years," she declared when she got home.

Charley grinned. "How many years?"

"Ninety-nine years," she answered grudgingly. You see, Ovie Wumpum had said May Cuddles was ninety-nine.

"Come back next year," she ordered. "I'll be a hundred then, for sure."

"I'll come back for a walk *tomorrow*," Charley Jarrow said. "I look forward to seeing you move again!"

The Thing

Timmy Summers was afraid that there was a *Thing* under his bed. Whenever his mom and dad turned out the light at night, he was sure that the Thing was waiting there in the dark. Of course, he had peeked. Slowly, quietly, he'd lowered himself down over the side of the mattress until at last he could see. But the Thing was too smart.

"He can make himself look like the wall," Tim told his dad.

"There is *nothing* under your bed," his dad repeated again and again. But Timmy knew better. He would tuck a flashlight under his covers, and then he'd wait for a sound—a creaking or a squeaking—and then he'd shine the flashlight. But the darned Thing was never caught in the beam. Once, Tim thought it was staring at him from the dark at the foot of the bed. Tim grabbed at it, but the Thing turned out to be his foot. Gosh, it was a clever Thing.

One night his mom told his uncle about the Thing, and she *laughed.* Timmy was embarrassed, but his uncle took it very seriously. "Don't laugh at the boy," he said to Timmy's mom. "These 'Things' can be very frightening to three-year-olds."

"I'll be *four* tomorrow," Timmy said.

"Oh, thank goodness," said his uncle. "Then this is the last night you have to worry abut the Thing. On your fourth birthday, the Thing goes away. If I were you, I'd sleep on the sofa in the living room tonight. Then tomorrow you can go back to your bed."

That's just what Timmy did. The next morning he woke up and was *four.* He never heard the Thing again.

That was his best birthday present!

Harry Boxer and the Kid

Most of the time, Harry Boxer lived in doorways, although some-times he lived under bridges, and occasionally behind garbage bins. His mother lived with him, collecting rags and old newspapers which she sold, now and then, for a tiny bit of money. Harry Boxer didn't remember *ever* living in a house, but his mother told him that when he was little, for a couple of years, they *had* lived in one. But Harry didn't care because although he had almost nothing, he and his mom had special times together.

When Harry was eight years old, not so long ago, he saw a sign in a store window that read: Wanted: Boy to deliver pizza. Must have bicycle.

Naturally, Harry didn't have a bicycle, but he *did* want that job. So

he spent days and days looking up and down every street in the city—and what do you know, he found a bike discarded in an alley. It was rusty and in terrible shape, but with some help from a couple of the men who also lived on the street, Harry got the tires patched and the frame unbent. They painted it red.

Harry jumped on his bicycle and rushed off to apply for the job at the pizza parlor. "Gee, I'm lucky," he thought as he pedaled. "I've got my mom, my bike, and soon I'll have a job."

On his way, Harry met another street kid, who thought that rebuilt bike was the greatest thing he'd ever seen. So Harry offered him a ride. "Gee," the kid said, "getting to ride on a bike! That's the best present I've gotten for my birthday."

"This is your birthday? How old are you?" Harry asked.

"Twelve, I think," the kid said.

"Don't you know? Why don't you ask your mother?" Harry said.

"Don't have one."

"You're kidding," Harry said. "Who takes care of you?"

"*I* take care of me," the kid said. He got off the bike and began to walk down the street.

"Hey, you! Wait!" shouted Harry. "This is for you." He pushed the bike at the kid and turned away. "They need a delivery boy at the pizza parlor," Harry said. "Happy Birthday, kid."

Harry ran home to his mother. He wished he could've given the kid more, but that was all he had. Actually, Harry had a whole lot more. He had heart. In fact, a lot of people in houses have a whole lot less than Harry Boxer.